FAVOURITE TALES

Rumpelstiltskin

illustrated
by
MARTIN AITCHISON

based on the story by Jacob and Wilhelm Grimm

Once there was a poor miller who had a beautiful daughter.

One day the King ordered him to come to the palace. The miller was very nervous as he stood before the King, and he said the first silly thing that came into his head. "My daughter can spin straw into gold!"

"Then bring her here at once!" said the King. "This I must see."

So the next day the foolish miller
brought his daughter to the palace.

The King put the girl in a tiny room.
"Here is some straw, and here is a
spinning wheel," he told her. "Spin
the straw into gold by morning, or you
shall die."

Locked in the tiny room, the miller's daughter wept to think of the impossible task before her. She had no idea how to spin straw into gold.

Suddenly the door flew open and in pranced a strange little man.

"I may be able to help you, Mistress Miller," he said.

"If you will give me your pretty glass necklace, I will spin the straw into gold before morning," the little man went on.

"Oh thank you!" gasped the miller's daughter.

The little man set to work. *Whirr!*
Whirr! Whirr! Three times round went
the spinning wheel as each reel was
filled.

In the morning, the King found only the miller's daughter and reels of golden thread.

"You have done very well indeed," he said. "But I wonder if you can perform the same trick twice. Tonight I shall give you more straw to spin, and we shall see what happens."

The miller's daughter was very frightened, but again the strange little man came to her rescue.

"Give me the ring from your finger," he said, "and I shall soon spin this straw into gold."

The little man set to work. *Whirr! Whirr! Whirr!* Three times round went the spinning wheel as each reel was filled.

In the morning, the King was very pleased to see the beautiful girl surrounded by reels of golden thread.

"Tonight you shall have even more straw to spin," he said. "If you spin it all into gold by morning, you shall be my queen."

This time, the miller's daughter cried more bitterly than ever.

"Why are you crying?" asked the little man when he appeared. "You know that I will help you."

"But I have nothing left to give you," sobbed the poor girl.

"If you become queen," the little man replied, "you can give me your first child."

Now the miller's daughter did not really believe that the King would marry her, so she agreed.

The little man set to work. *Whirr! Whirr! Whirr!* Three times round went the spinning wheel as each reel was filled.

The next day, when he saw all the
golden thread, the King was
delighted. The miller's daughter had
brought him great riches, and she
really was very beautiful. So the King
kept his promise and married her.

Everyone was thrilled – especially the proud miller!

The new Queen was very happy, and she forgot all about the strange little man. Before long, she and the King had a beautiful baby.

Suddenly, late one night, the little man appeared in the Queen's bedroom. "I have come for the child you promised me," he said, grinning.

The Queen was horrified. "Please don't take my baby," she begged. "Take all my gold and jewels instead!"

"No," said the little man. "In three nights' time, I shall take the child...unless you can discover my real name."

The desperate Queen sent messengers throughout the kingdom to collect all the names they could find.

The following night, and the night after, she repeated all the names to the little man. He just laughed and laughed.

"That is not my name!" he said, over and over.

On the third day, the Queen begged her messengers for more names. At last one of them told her of how, deep in the forest, he had seen a strange little man dancing and singing,

"The Queen will never win my game,
For Rumpelstiltskin is my name!"

The Queen was overjoyed.

When the little man arrived that night, the Queen pretended to think hard.

"Is your name Twinkletoes?" she asked.

"No!" said the little man. "That is not my name!"

"Is your name Shagribanda, then?"

"Ha, ha! No, that is not my name!"

"Or are you called... *Rumpelstiltskin*?"

At that the little man stamped his foot in fury and vanished. And you know, he has never been seen again from that day to this.